Leyla Winton is a young author, born and raised in San Rafael, California. At just 15 years old she wrote her first published book, Underwater Drama Class, although she's been writing stories since first grade. As someone who has anxiety and is neurodiverse, she is very passionate about mental health issues, especially in young kids. She wrote Underwater Drama Class for young people to relate to and know that it does get better. She is currently writing a screenplay she hopes will take off!

UNDERWATER DRAMA CLASS

LEYLA WINTON

AUSTIN MACAULEY PUBLISHERS™
LONDON • CAMBRIDGE • NEW YORK • SHARJAH

Ordering Information
Quantity sales: Special discounts are available on quantity purchases by corporations, associations, and others. For details, contact the publisher at the address below.

Publisher's Cataloging-in-Publication data
Winton, Leyla
Underwater Drama Class

ISBN 9781685622183 (Paperback)
ISBN 9781685622190 (Hardback)
ISBN 9781685622206 (ePub e-book)

Library of Congress Control Number: 2023905075

www.austinmacauley.com/us

First Published 2023
Austin Macauley Publishers LLC
40 Wall Street, 33rd Floor, Suite 3302
New York, NY 10005
USA

mail-usa@austinmacauley.com
+1 (646) 5125767

Dedicated to anyone who has ever struggled with anxiety.

Thank you to Eric, who helped spark my inspiration for this book. Thank you to my parents, Matt and Ramina, and siblings, Nineveh and Elias, who have supported me every step of the way. Thank you to Kiara and Drew who never complained when I made them read my drafts and talked their ears off about plots and characters. Thank you to my entire family for loving and supporting me.

Heidi took a deep breathe before stepping through the school's doorway. "Don't worry, Heidi, the first day of school is always a little scary!" Heidi's mother gave her a kiss and shooed her through the door.

Heidi scurried to the back of the classroom where she hid in her shell. Other students shuffled into the room and sat down. They were all chatting with each other, except for Heidi.

Finally, the teacher walked in and smiled at the kids. "Good morning, students, and welcome to your first day of drama class! My name is Ms. Seaweed and this year, we will learn how to be more confident on and off stage! I look forward to seeing you all shine in the spotlight!" All the kids cheered, except for Heidi. "Settle down, class, we won't get anything done unless we begin! So, who's ready for the first assignment?" The whole class raised their hands, except for Heidi. If anything, she hid further in her shell.

8

Ms. Seaweed didn't seem to notice Heidi hiding in the back row, for she smiled brightly and went on with her lesson. "Great!" she exclaimed. "Your first task will be to learn a scene from the classic play, Remora and Jewelfish! Here are your lines." Ms. Seaweed passed out pieces of kelp with their lines written in octopus ink. "Now, it's snack time! Go grab your lunchboxes and eat your snack outside."

All the kids ran outside, laughing and talking, while Heidi slowly made her way to the door. She grabbed her lunchbox and sat against the wall, watching the other kids running and playing. When the conch shell sounded, everyone stampeded to the classroom door, nearly trampling poor Heidi.

Once all the kids were back in class, Ms. Seaweed took them through the lines together. "It is only the name of my rival, it is myself although I am not a remora fish. What is a remora, if it is still only a fish? Why must you be a remora? If I could be any fish, I would choose to be a remora, only to be with you."

After running through the lines together, Ms. Seaweed began to call on the students to say the lines.

Ms. Seaweed pointed to Heidi, but Heidi just froze. She couldn't speak, even if she wanted to. Ms. Seaweed nodded, trying to get Heidi to talk, but Heidi just stood still. Ms. Seaweed sighed and moved on, although the other students whispered to each other, occasionally looking back at poor Heidi.

The next day at snack time, Heidi sat alone again, but this time, some of the other kids made fun of her for freezing up in class. A small starfish stood in front of Heidi and yelled at the other kids, "Stop teasing her! It's not nice." The kids just laughed and walked away, but the starfish sat down next to Heidi. "My name is Bubble, what's yours?"

Heidi just blinked. She finally whispered, "My name's Heidi."

Bubble smiled and stuck out her hand. "Nice to meet you, Heidi!" Heidi smiled shyly and shook Bubble's extended hand.

After snack that day, Bubble held Heidi back so she didn't get stepped on. They walked into class together, and Bubble sat with Heidi in the back.

Heidi smiled at Bubble as Ms. Seaweed began to talk. "We will spend the rest of today memorizing the lines and the rest of the week will be dedicated to your performances. Heidi, would you like to start us off?"

Heidi shook her head, but Bubble nudged her. She whispered, "You can do this!"

Heidi took a deep breath and recited quietly, "I-It is the name of m-my rival, it is myself although I-I am not a remora fish." Ms. Seaweed beamed, but the other kids snickered at Heidi's stutter. Bubble noticed Heidi start to hide in her shell, so she stood up and finished the lines for Heidi, making

sure her new friend wasn't
too embarrassed. Heidi smiled
thankfully at Bubble as Ms.
Seaweed moved on.
"Thanks, Bubble." Heidi poked her
head out of her shell a little.

When it was time for Heidi's performance two days later, Bubble spent all of snack time helping Heidi prepare. After running through the lines ten times, Bubble beamed. "I think you're ready, Heidi! You're going to prove everyone wrong, I know you will!" Heidi sighed and smiled back at Bubble. "Thanks for all your help, I'm really grateful for you." Heidi stood up and walked back to the classroom with Bubble. Ms. Seaweed called Heidi up to the stage in front of the classroom.

Heidi took a deep breath and saw Bubble smiling at her, but she also saw the other kids whispering and laughing. Bubble pointed at her eyes, trying to tell Heidi to focus on her. Looking straight at Bubble, Heidi stretched her neck out of her shell and began to recite the lines. "It is only the name of my rival, it is myself although I am not a remora fish. What is a remora, if it is still only a fish? Why must you be a remora? If I could be any fish, I would choose to be a remora, only to be with you." She exhaled and looked at Ms. Seaweed, who had a huge smile on her face, then to her classmates, who were in pure shock. Bubble started to clap, and others started to clap too. Soon, everyone was on their feet, cheering as loud as they could for Heidi. She blushed and scurried back to her seat next to Bubble.

"You were amazing! I'm so proud of you, Heidi!" Bubble held her hand up for a high-five, which Heidi returned gladly. "I couldn't have done it without you, Bubble. Thank you so much!" Heidi giggled and sat back in her chair.

The next day, everyone was whispering in a circle when Heidi got to class. She wondered what was going on. Were they talking about her? Just then, Bubble noticed Heidi and she shushed everyone in the circle. She walked away from everyone else and towards Heidi. She cleared her throat and said, "Heidi, we are all so proud of you for getting on stage and performing, so because you came out of your shell, we made a new one for you!" Ms. Seaweed separated herself from the group, holding a brand new shell that had glittering stars all over it.

"This is for you, Heidi!" She presented Heidi with the new shell, and Heidi began to cry.

"It's beautiful! No one's ever made me a shell before, thank you all!" Heidi crawled out of her old shell and into the new one. Everyone cheered for their new friend and her sparkling shell.

THE END

CPSIA information can be obtained
at www.ICGtesting.com
Printed in the USA
LVHW011323220623
750479LV00003B/40